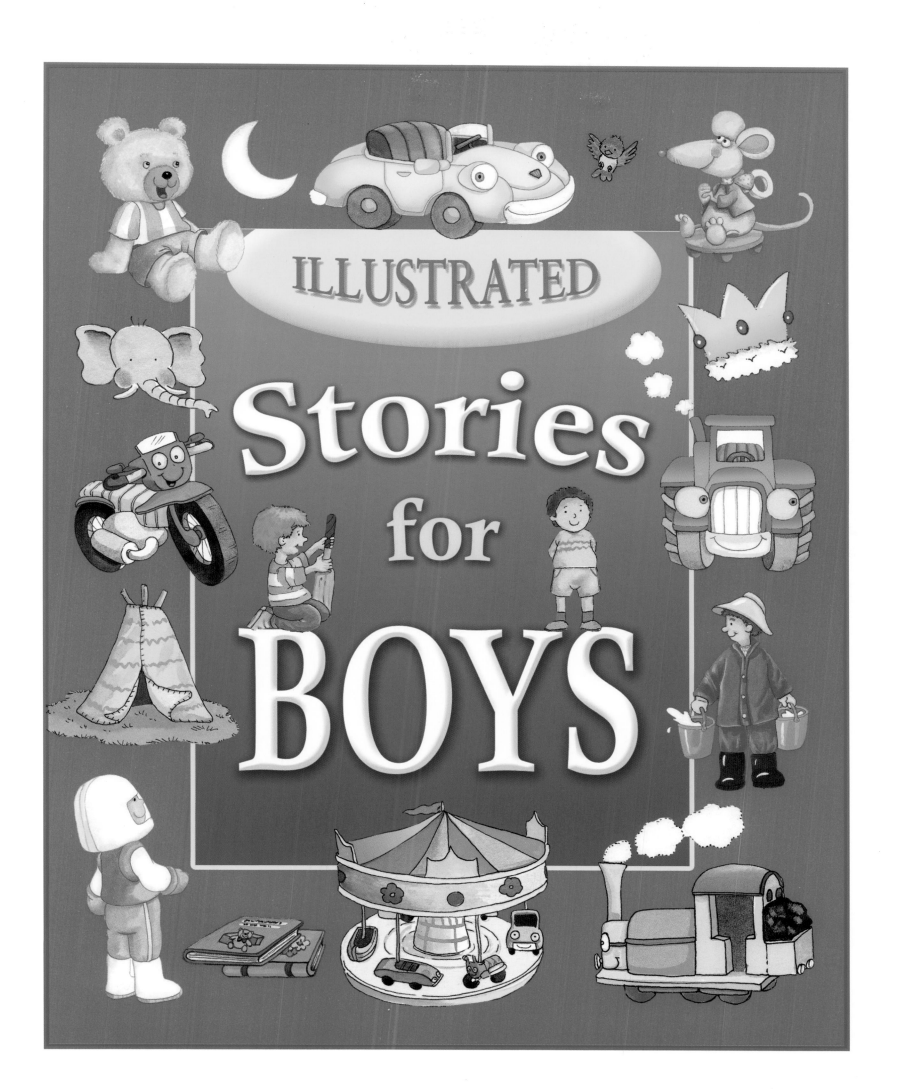

ILLUSTRATED

Stories for BOYS

Brown Watson
ENGLAND

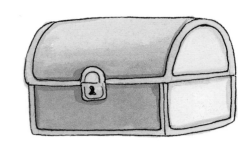

CONTENTS

TUBBY AND SPEEDY

Tubby the Tractor did not go very fast. Speedy the sports car was always teasing him.

'Hoot! Hoot!' he hooted, speeding down the lane. 'See how I race along!'

'Stop!' cried Farmer Bell. 'You have made my chickens run off!'

'You have scared the sheep!' said Tubby. But Speedy did not care.

It began to rain. For the rest of the day and all night, it rained hard. Next day Tubby had to go even slower across the muddy ground.

'Poor old Tubby!' hooted Speedy. 'I can go fast, rain or no rain!' SPLASH! Speedy went right into a big puddle, drenching the sheep in muddy water! 'Hoot! Hoot!' hooted Speedy. 'Hoot! Hoot!' The rain had made the lane very wet and VERY slippery. Speedy was going much too fast…

'HOOT!' Now, Speedy was slipping and skidding. He tried to slow down. He tried to stop.

'Look out!' shouted Farmer Bell. 'The pond!' But it was too late.

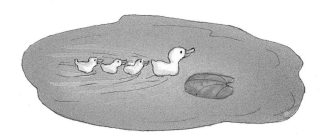

SPLASH! Now, Speedy was drenched in water! 'Come on, Tubby,' said Farmer Bell. He drove him to the edge of the pond. Then he tied one end of a rope to Tubby's tow bar and the other end to Speedy's bumper.

'Now!' said Farmer Bell. 'Pull!' Tubby did enjoy pulling Speedy out of the pond! Towing him back down the lane was even more fun!

'Hoot! Hoot!' went Tubby the Tractor. 'Now I am going MUCH faster than you, Speedy!'

SPACEMAN AND BABY BEAR

Spaceman was at the window, looking out at the night sky.

'I do not like night-time!' said Baby Bear. 'I hate the dark.'

'The night is not ALL dark!' said Spaceman. 'Come and see how brightly the moon shines!'

So Baby Bear went to the window. 'Those stars are so bright!' he said. 'Is that what you look at every night, Spaceman?'

'Yes,' said Spaceman. 'I hope I might see a spaceship, too!'

'What is a spaceship like?' said Baby Bear. 'Is it like a bright, shiny bubble with bright lights?'

'That is right!' said Spaceman. 'How did you know?'

'There is one right there!' cried Baby Bear, pointing. He was right!

The spaceship came closer, its lights flashing. A bright beam of light closed in around Spaceman and Baby Bear. Then, they were in the spaceship! The light from the moon and the stars made the sky as bright as day. What a fantastic sight!

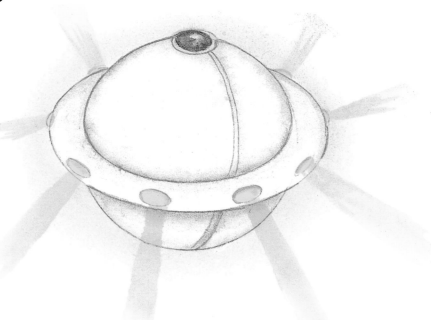

'I have dreamt of this every night!' Spaceman kept saying. 'Now, it is beginning to get light. Night is coming to an end.'

As he spoke a beam of light inside the spaceship became so bright that he and Baby Bear had to close their eyes tight. When they opened them again, they were back in the house, looking out of the window!

'What a flight!' said Spaceman. 'Are you all right, Baby Bear?'

But Baby Bear was already fast asleep, dreaming of spaceships!

HIDE AND SEEK!

'Let's play Hide and Seek!' said Giraffe.

'Yes-s-s...' hissed Snake. 'Seeking is easy for you, Giraffe, with your long neck and tall legs!' 'I agree!' said Zebra.

'Then I will hide!' said Giraffe. 'One of you can do the seeking!'

'Sounds fun!' roared Tiger Cub. And off he ran. He hid behind a bush. But the sun cast his shadow on the ground. So, he laid down in the shade of a tree and waited.

Then, Tiger Cub got up and looked around. As he crept forward, he saw black and white shadows. Yet there was no sun! 'Zebra!' he roared. 'Come out from behind that bush!'

'You found me, Tiger Cub!' said Zebra. 'Well done!'

Next, Tiger Cub saw blossom hanging from the branches of a tree. He looked down at the trunk.

'Blossom does not grow on the trunk!' he roared. 'It is YOU, Snake, curled round and round!'

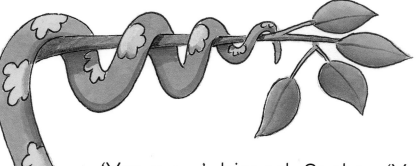

'Yes-s-s...' hissed Snake. 'You found me, Tiger Cub! Well done!'

'And only a tall tree can hide a tall Giraffe!' Tiger Cub went on. 'Come out, Giraffe!'

'You found me, Tiger Cub!' said Giraffe. 'Well done!'

'Yes!' roared Tiger Cub. 'But nobody came to find ME!'

'But YOU were the seeker!' said Zebra. 'Well done, Tiger Cub!'

'Let us have another game!' said Tiger Cub. 'And I really WILL be hiding this time!'

DON AND BIGGER DIGGER

Don the Digger had come to dig a sandpit at Barn School.

'Huh!' snorted Bigger Digger.

'A sandpit! I will be digging a road!'

'Our school is where Farmer Day's family home used to be,' Miss Foot was saying.

'And I do wish I was able to show you what it was like when I was a boy!' said Farmer Day.

Don went on digging. Then – CLANG!

'Hah!' said Bigger Digger. 'You are in trouble now!'

'Don hit an old, tin trunk,' said his driver. 'It was under the ground!'

'Grandad's trunk!' said Farmer Day. 'So that is where it was!'

Don scooped out the trunk. It was damp and rusty, but Farmer Day managed to lift the lid. So many things were inside!

'Grandma's milking stool!' cried Farmer Day. 'And the yoke she used to carry the pails of milk! Grandad's wind-up gramophone! And all these pictures!'

And that was not all.

There were toys and games, hoops and sticks, even some clothes!

'I want Barn School to have these things,' said Farmer Day. 'I wanted you to see how things used to be. Now I have my wish.'

'So, Don grants wishes!' said his driver. The children cheered.

'Don found the tin trunk!' said Miss Foot, happily.

'Don is a GREAT digger!' cried Farmer Day.

And Bigger Digger? He said nothing at all.

19

THE LOST SQUEAK!

Squeaky Snake had lost his squeak!

Robot banged him on the back. Fairy squeezed him tight. But his squeak had not come back. Sadly, Squeaky wandered about. Suddenly he heard the thump of big feet. He looked up to see two tusks and a long, grey trunk among the thick, green plants.

'Am I in the jungle?' gasped Squeaky.

'A balcony is as good as a jungle for an elephant without a trumpet noise,' came a voice.

'A trumpet noise?' said Squeaky. 'Was it like this?' He blew on a whistle. A tinny sound came out.

'No,' smiled Elephant. 'That is not like my trumpet noise.'

'Was it like this?' said Squeaky. He blew on a bubble pipe. A bubbly sound came out.

'No,' Elephant smiled again. 'That is not like my trumpet noise!'

'Was it like this?' said Squeaky. He took a balloon and blew and blew until – BANG! The balloon burst! And Squeaky gave a squeak!

'SQUEAK! My squeak is back!' he cried. 'Squeak! SQUEAK!'

But, Elephant was laughing too much to listen! 'Ha-ha! HA-HA!' Then, 'Tara-Tara! TARA-TARA!'

'SQUEAK!' went Squeaky. 'You have got your trumpet noise back!'

'TARA-TARA!' went Elephant.

'You have got your squeak back!'

Now, just to make sure that Squeaky can squeak and Elephant can make a trumpet noise, they make each other laugh! SQUEAK-SQUEAK! TARA-TARA!

FIRE ENGINE FRED

Fire Engine Fred was at the Town Show. 'Can I work the hose?' asked a boy.

'There is no fire!' said Fireman Tim. 'You can sound the bell instead!'

CLANG-CLANG! The boy enjoyed ringing Fred's bell! But Fred DID wish that there WAS a fire to put out!

All the way back to the fire station, Fred kept thinking about putting out a real fire. Then he saw a tall swirl of black smoke…

23

'Fire!' shouted Fireman Bill, clanging the bell. 'There is a fire at Betty Baker's cottage!'

Fred raced to the cottage.

'Get the hose, Bill!' said Tim. 'Fix it to the water-tap and aim it at the window! I am going inside!'

There was smoke inside the cottage!

'Betty!' cried Tim.

'Let me carry you into the garden, away from the fire!'

'There is NO fire!' cried Betty. 'I burnt some bread, so I opened the window to let the smoke out!'

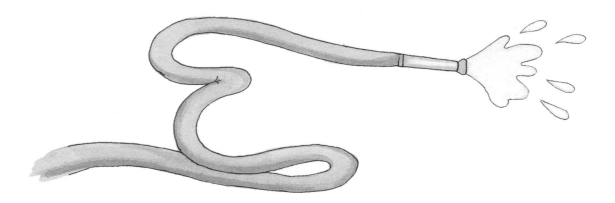

Poor Tim! 'We have soaked your kitchen with water from Fred's hose!' he said. 'I am so sorry.'

Betty smiled. 'Fred is enjoying the sunshine!' she said. 'Bring my things out here to dry and then we can do the same! We can all have some of the cakes I have baked!'

'We are glad you did not have a real fire!' said Bill.

'So am I!' said Betty. 'And it is good to know that you and Fire Engine Fred are always ready to help when people need you!'

THE KING AND THE WIZARD

'Oh, dear!' King Cole said to his servant, Sam. 'Wizard Woo teases the children. He makes cats bark and dogs quack! Now, he has just sent this message!' Sam began to read aloud.

'I will come to the palace today to see King Cole. If he can tell me the first thing I am thinking, I shall go away for ever! If not, I shall be king!'

'If only Wizard Woo DID go away for good!' said the king.

Sam was looking at the king's crown and his red velvet robe.

'Oh, dear!' said King Cole. 'Do something, Sam!' Sam called a footman. 'Bring Wizard Woo to me when he arrives!' he said. 'Sam!' said the king. 'How can you smile at a time like this?'

Wizard Woo also smiled when he arrived, seeing the crown and the red velvet gown. 'King Cole!' said Wizard Woo. 'Can you tell me the first thing I am thinking?'

'You think I am King Cole!' came the reply. 'That is the first thing you were thinking! True?'

'Yes,' said the wizard, 'but…'

Off came the crown and the robe. It was Sam! 'And you were thinking I was the king!' he said.

Wizard Woo flew into a rage!

'You have made me look a fool!' he cried. 'I am going!' And off he went.

'Peace at last!' said King Cole. 'My crown, please, Sam!'

'Of course!' smiled Sam.

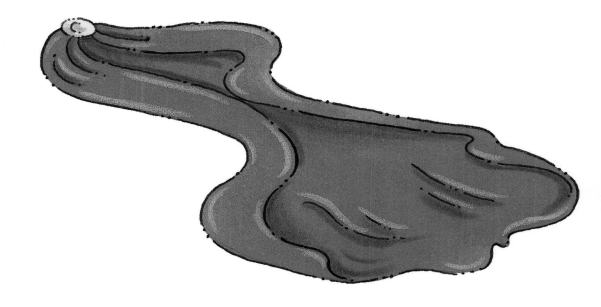

MONTY ON THE MOVE

Monty had been a fine motorbike, crowds cheering as he raced around the track. 'Good old Monty!' 'Monty wins!' Then came the day when his wheels stopped turning. 'No more races, Monty,' said Keith, his rider. 'You are going to a theme park!' At the theme park there was a little railway, a boating lake, model cars… and a museum.

'This is your new home, Monty!' said Keith. 'In you go!'

But how Monty hated the idea of just standing still, getting rusty!

'Hey!' came a voice. 'Look at that motorbike!' A boy got into the saddle and gripped Monty's handlebars. 'Brrm, brrm!' he said.

'Get off, Max!' said the boy's dad. But other children wanted to climb up on Monty, too!

'Brrm, brrm! Brrm, brrm!' 'My turn next!' 'Good old Monty!' Then two mechanics came and wheeled Monty away. 'This bike is just what we needed!' one said.

Monty did not hear them. He was dreaming that he was a fine motorbike once more, crowds cheering. 'Good old Monty!' 'Monty wins!'

Hands gripped his handlebars. Someone was sitting in his saddle, and then – 'Brrm, brrm!'

'Look at me on the motorbike!' someone shouted. 'He is the best thing on this roundabout. Hurrah!'

'Better than him standing still and getting rusty!' said the mechanics.

Now, Monty is on the move all day long! Brrm, brrm!

JACK-IN-THE-BOX KNOCKS!

Jack-in-the-Box was inside his box! 'Let me out!' he shouted.

Clown undid the catch. Then – boing! Up jumped Jack!

'Waah!' cried Baby Bear. 'He makes me jump!'

'Whee!' squeaked Clockwork Mouse. 'He makes me squeal!'

'Whooo!' went Spinning Top. 'He makes me hum!'

'Back inside the box, Jack!' said Clown. 'You frighten the toys!'

Poor Jack! Clown did feel sad.

He tapped on the box. 'Jack!' he called. 'Are you all right?'

'Yes!' shouted Jack-in-the-Box.

Clown did not hear him. 'Jack!' he shouted again. 'Are you all right?'

'Yes!' shouted Jack again.

Still Clown did not hear. 'Jack!' he shouted. 'Are you all right?'

'Is Clown talking to himself?' asked Spaceman. 'We must find out!' So the toys went closer.

'Jack!' Clown shouted again. He knocked on the box. Jack knocked back. Knock! Knock!

'Jack knocks!' said Clown. 'Out of the box!' He undid the catch and out jumped Jack-in-the-Box!

All the toys cheered!

'Again!' cried Baby Bear. 'Do it again!' So back went Jack into the box. Then – Knock! Knock!

'Jack knocks!' cried Clown. 'Out of the box!' And up jumped Jack.

Now, all the toys like hearing Jack knock. 'Jack knocks! Out of the box!' they cry. And up jumps Jack-in-the-Box.

BOING!

THEY LAUGHED AND LAUGHED!

The jungle animals were putting on a show! 'We can tap dance!' said the hippos. They stood on their hind legs, hooves tapping. Tap, tap, tap! Such fine 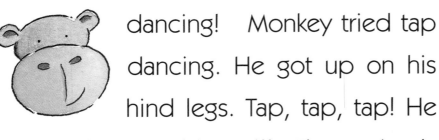 dancing! Monkey tried tap dancing. He got up on his hind legs. Tap, tap, tap! He tripped over his tail! The animals laughed and laughed. Crocodile rolled balls of mud along his tail. He tossed the balls into the air, ready to catch on his snout. Such fine juggling!

Monkey tried juggling. He tossed a ball into the air. It fell – SPLAT! – all over his face. The animals laughed and laughed! The elephants made trumpet sounds with their trunks. Ta-ra! Ta-ra! Such fine trumpeting! Monkey tried making trumpet sounds. He puffed out his cheeks and blew. But no sound came out! The animals laughed and laughed.

Snakes bent themselves into strange shapes. Then they curled up in coils. Such fine contortions!

Monkey tried to do contortions. He put one arm around his head. Next, he curled one leg around his back. Then he tried putting his other leg behind his neck. BUMP! Monkey fell over.

'I cannot do contortions!' said poor Monkey. 'I cannot make trumpet sounds. I cannot juggle. I cannot tap dance. What CAN I do?' How the animals laughed!

'You make us laugh and laugh!' they said. 'Monkey, you are the funny clown, star of our show!'

NO LEAVES ON THE LINE

Eddie liked being a steam engine, even though he only pulled trucks on a goods line. Dennis the Diesel pulled the trains on the main line.

'How slow you are!' he snorted at Eddie. 'Still, you only pull trucks!'

'I am as good as you are!' Eddie puffed. But Dennis whizzed past.

The days began to get shorter. The leaves were beginning to fall.

'More coal in your fire-box, Eddie!' said Dave, his driver. 'We need lots of steam today!'

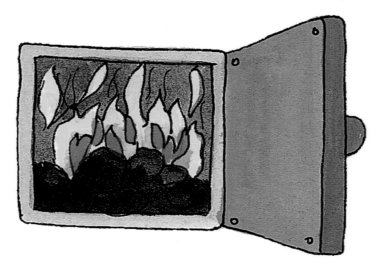

'Coal!' cried Dennis. 'Steam! Hah!'

Eddie was just getting up steam, when there was a loud screech.

'Sounds like Dennis is in trouble on the main line!' said Dave. 'And just listen to those passengers!'

The passengers were very cross!

'Why has the train stopped?'

'What is wrong with the engine?'

'Fallen leaves are clogging up the line!' said the driver. 'The engine cannot move!'

A man pointed at Eddie. 'That engine is moving!' he said.

43

'The sparks from Eddie's fire-box burn up leaves as soon as they fall!' said Dave. 'Leaves on the line are no problem for us!'

'Then Eddie can pull our train!' said an important-looking man. 'I am a director of the railway!'

So Dennis was shunted away and Eddie puffed down the line, burning all the leaves as he went.

'Hurrah!' cried the passengers.

'Hurrah!' puffed Eddie.

And if Dennis did say anything, nobody heard him.

MONSTER MOUSE

Clockwork Mouse hated not being seen by the other toys!

'Nearly trod on your tail!' said Robot. 'I did not see you!'

'Sorry I bumped into you!' said Spinning Top. 'I did not see you!'

'Sorry I did not say hello!' said Blue Rabbit. 'I did not see you!'

One day, Clockwork Mouse found a mask. He put his wheels inside and it flipped up in front of him. What an ugly monster face!

'Help!' cried Dolly. 'A monster!'

Clockwork Mouse gave a little squeak. The toys were sure to see him now! He tried a monster voice.

'Whooo! I am a monster!'

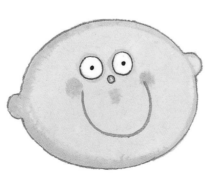

'Help!' wailed Blue Rabbit. 'There is a monster in here!'

'Whooo!' went Clockwork Mouse again. 'I am a monster!'

'Help!' screamed Baby Bear. 'There is a monster in here!' He sounded so frightened that Clockwork Mouse felt mean.

'Wait!' he cried. He tried to get out of the mask, but he couldn't. He was wedged tightly inside.

'A monster!' cried Fairy. 'Help!'

Clockwork Mouse wriggled. He jiggled. Then he pulled. Off came the mask. Robot spoke first.

'Some monster! Clockwork Mouse and a monster mask!'

'Sorry if I frightened you,' said Clockwork Mouse. 'But I wanted to be seen!' He looked so sorry for himself that the toys smiled.

'Well,' said Clown, 'it is nice to know that there is not a REAL monster in here, after all!'

THE BARBECUE DRAGON

When Dilly the Dragon roared, flames came out of his mouth.

Then, it started to rain and Dilly got cold. There was no roar. No flames.

'My fire is out!' he said. 'I must breathe air to make flames. There is plenty of fresh air in the forest!'

In the forest there was a notice – BEWARE OF FIRE. 'Very wise,' said Dilly. 'But I need MY fire!' Another notice said – FIRE CAUSES DAMAGE. 'True,' said Dilly. 'But I NEED my fire!'

Another notice said – PUT FIRES OUT! Poor Dilly felt so cold!

'No fires, today!' a voice was saying. 'It is too cold and damp!'

'So, can we have our barbecue party, Linda?' a girl called out.

'I do not think so, Penny' said Linda. 'It is raining again! Quick! We must shelter in the forest!'

Dilly went over to the barbecue. It was still warm. He breathed in, feeling warmer inside. Just as the rain stopped – R-OA-OA-RR! – flames came out of his mouth!

'What was that?' a boy called out. 'It sounded like thunder!' Everyone went to see.

'There is a fire for our barbecue!' cried Penny. 'We can have our party!'

'That dragon helped us!' said Holly. 'He roared like thunder and breathed flames! I saw him!'

'Dragons?' said Linda. 'Dragons are only for story books, Holly!'

'But I DID see him!' said Holly with a smile. 'Really, I did!' And just then, Dilly let out another roar.

R-OA-OA-RR!

BOB'S HEAVY LOAD

'My truck has broken down!' said Tina, the potter. 'It is loaded up!'

'Bob the Breakdown Van will tow it back to your studio,' said Al. 'You can unload your things and leave it outside. We will tow it to my garage tomorrow.'

It was hard work pulling Tina's truck with such a heavy load. Bob looked forward to it being empty! Next day, a man came with some clay for Tina. 'I will put this in her truck,' he said to himself.

Bob did not know about the clay. He only knew the truck felt heavy!

Al put on the brakes. As Bob stopped, apples fell from a tree and into Tina's truck! Now, Bob's load felt even heavier!

Men were cutting logs. 'More odd branches, Pete!' one shouted. He threw them across and they landed in Tina's truck! 'Where do you want these sacks, Mack?' said Pete.

'In the truck!' cried Mack. But Pete threw them into Tina's truck!

By now, Bob's load was so heavy, he was glad to get to Al's garage.

'See what was in Tina's truck!' said Al. 'Clay, apples, bundles of branches and a pile of sacks. Sacks are just what we need!'

'Apples!' cried Al's son, Jay. 'And I need branches for my wigwam!'

'I need that clay!' came Tina's voice. 'The man from the clay-works said it was in my truck!'

'And apples, branches and sacks!' said Jay. 'And Bob the Breakdown Van pulled the whole load!'

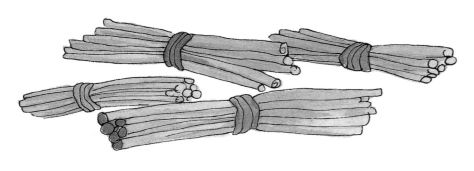

WE LOVE HATTIE!

Hattie the Helicopter was landing at a big airport. 'Steady, Hattie,' said Roy, her pilot.

'We have fetched roses from Star Island!' Roy told a lady officer.

'Just in time for the visit by the Group Captain!' said the lady. 'Please stay and have a rest!'

'I never rest!' snorted a jumbo jet. 'And I fly around the world!'

'I have rescued people at sea,' said Hattie. 'And I have landed in the jungle!'

'Sssh!' came a voice. 'Here is the Group Captain!'

The Captain looked splendid in his uniform. 'Star Island roses!' he said. 'Look, Posy and Tim!'

'Oh, Grandpa,' said Tim. 'We wanted to go up in an aeroplane!' 'But these aircraft need a lot of fuel to make them go,' said Captain. 'And they need lots of space to take off.' Then he saw Hattie. 'A helicopter!' he said. 'Now, that needs no space at all to take off. What about fuel, pilot?'

'Plenty in the tank, sir!' said Roy.

'Then let's go!' said the Captain. They got inside. Hattie's rotor blades whirred, taking them up into the sky.

'There is Star Island!' said the Captain. 'Steady, Hattie!'

Roy flew Hattie all around Star Island before landing back at the airport. 'That was great, Grandpa!' said Tim. 'Thank you!'

'You must thank Hattie!' said the Captain. 'She made it happen!'

'Yes!' said Posy. 'We LOVE Hattie the Helicopter!'

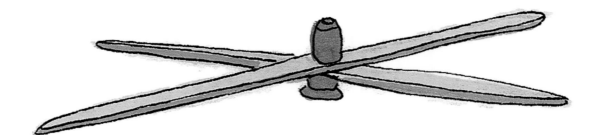

MITCH, THE MAILVAN

Mitch the mailvan had almost finished work. When the day began, he had been loaded up with letters, cards, parcels and packets. Now, there was one parcel left.

'Who is this for, Mitch?' asked Dave. 'The label is torn. I can only read Mi... I know! It must be for Miss Dixon, the baker!'

But the parcel was not for Miss Dixon. 'So, who is it for?' said Dave. 'I can only read Mi...'

'I think I know!' said Miss Dixon.

And off she went without another word.

'Mi..' read Dave again. 'Who is this for, Mitch? I know! It must be Mike Bond at the garage!'

But the parcel was not for Mike.

'So, who is it for?' said Dave. 'Look! I can just make out Mi...'

'I think I know!' said Mike. And off he went without another word.

'Mi..' said Dave, trying to read the label again. 'Who is this for, Mitch? I know! It must be Mill Lane School!'

But the parcel was not for Mill Lane School.

'So, who is it for?' said Dave.

Then, Mitch saw Miss Dixon and Mike Bond, together with all the children at Mill Lane School.

'Open it!' they shouted all together. 'Open the parcel!'

So, Dave opened the parcel. And inside was a shiny new name-plate with the name 'MITCH' on it.

'Well, well!' smiled Dave. 'Now, we know who the parcel was for!'

First published 2008 by Brown Watson
The Old Mill, 76 Fleckney Road
Kibworth Beauchamp
Leicestershire LE8 0HG

ISBN: 978-0-7097-1829-1

Reprinted 2009, 2010, 2011
Printed in Malaysia